Hardie Grant acknowledges the Traditional Owners of the Country on which we work, the Wurundjeri People of the Kulin Nation and the Gadigal People of the Eora Nation, and recognises their continuing connection to the land, waters and culture. We pay our respects to their Elders past and present.

Bright Light
an imprint of Hardie Grant Children's Publishing
Wurundjeri Country
Ground Floor, Building 1, 658 Church Street
Richmond, Victoria 3121, Australia
Melbourne | Sydney | San Francisco
www.hardiegrantchildrens.com

Australia, New Zealand & UK ISBN: 9781761212963
North America ISBN: 9781761213748
First published 2024

Part of the author's proceeds of this book go toward the Pink Elephants Support Network, a not-for-profit charity formed to support women through miscarriage, pregnancy loss and beyond.

 A catalogue record for this book is available from the National Library of Australia

Publisher Marisa Pintado **Design** Pooja Desai
Editorial Joanna Wong with Johanna Gogos **Production** Amanda Shaw

With thanks to Tammy Court-Cudd, LMSW, Grief Therapist, and Certified Thanatologist, for her guidance.

Printed in China by Leo Paper Group

 The paper this book is printed on is from FSC®-certified forests and other sources. FSC® promotes environmentally responsible, socially beneficial and economically viable management of the world's forests.

GROW BIG, LITTLE SEED

A story about rainbow babies

Bec Nanayakkara   Sarah Capon

Bright Light
Hardie Grant Children's Publishing

For all families, everywhere.
Though the journey is not always easy,
I pray it will always be blessed. – BN

To my parents — who lovingly grew
their little seeds too. – SC

Exciting things were happening in Nina's home.

'While we wait,' said Mom, 'let's plant a seed and watch it grow.'

Nina made a space in the earth
and placed her treasure inside.

'Grow big, little seed,'
she said.

Nina hoped big hopes and dreamed big dreams for her little seed.

The seed began to grow.

Nina held back storms,

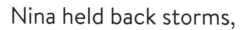

blew breezes,

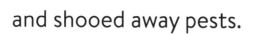

and shooed away pests.

Most importantly, she made sure
her plant was never lonely.

But one day, Nina's plant began to droop.

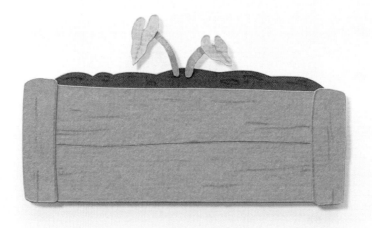

Its leaves turned brown

and it grew no more.

'I don't understand,' said Nina,
'I did everything I could!'

'Sometimes,' said Mom,
'even when we do all that
we can, things don't go
the way we hoped.'

'We can try again?' said Dad.

But Nina shook her head.

Days grew into weeks, and weeks grew into seasons.

In the fall, Nina found gold.

But she didn't plant another seed.

In winter, Nina spread her wings.

But she didn't plant another seed.

In spring, Nina saved lives.

But she *still* didn't plant another seed.

Then summer came, and
a day-dreamy breeze drifted by.

It whispered words that made Nina feel
as if anything might be possible ...

So, Nina made a space in the earth
and placed her new treasure inside.

'Grow big, little seed,'
she said.

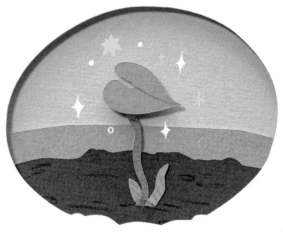

The seed began to grow.

Nina held back storms,

blew breezes,

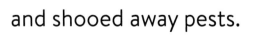

and shooed away pests.

Most importantly, she made sure
her plant always had company.

And this time,

it grew,

and **grew,**

and
GREW,
until ...

It grew bigger *and* better than all of Nina's hopes and dreams.

Which was just as well.

Because everyone loved pumpkin.